A Bestiary of My Heart
Cautionary Tales

Victoria Nelson

InkerMen Press
2011

A Bestiary of My Heart
Cautionary Tales
by
Victoria Nelson

Victoria Nelson © 2011

This edition copyright © InkerMen Press 2011

Cover illustration *Woman in Feathered Cape*, 1999, pencil, gouache, stitched fabric on linen, by Deborah Barrett.

Type design with thanks to Jack Werner Stauffacher, The Greenwood Press, San Francisco.

Written over a thirty-year period, a number of these stories began as dreams. Versions have appeared in the journals *Raritan, Southwest Review, Agni, Women's Studies,* and *Hawaii Review;* in Rebis Press limited edition and in *Ovid Metamorphosed* (Chatto & Windus, 2000). Sigiriya from *Gypsy Cante: Deep Song of the Caves,* translated by Will Kirkland. Copyright ©1999 by Will Kirkland. Reprinted by permission of City Lights Books.

This is a work of fiction.
Any resemblance to persons living or dead is purely coincidental.

InkerMen Press, Ashby-de-la-Zouch
info@inkermenpress.co.uk
www.inkermenpress.co.uk

978-0-9562749-2-2

British Library Cataloguing in Publication Data

Nelson, Victoria, 1945-
    A bestiary of my heart : cautionary tales.
    I. Title
    813.6-dc23
ISBN-13: 9780956274922

A Bestiary of My Heart
Cautionary Tales

Victoria Nelson

Contents

Main Train Station	9
Head of the President (Five True Tales)	11
Draculess	18
Loglines (A Love Story)	27
Rose Canyon Adventure	28
One Million B.C. (The Prehistory of Love)	32
Halawa Valley Slide Show	47
Four Oahu Tales	51
Dead Lover	56
Two Women	67
Blonde Is Blonde (But Silver Runs Deep)	82
Wild Child	86
If the Earth Quakes	92
Jacob's Ladder	93
A Bestiary of My Heart	100

A yorá mis penas
Me fui a un olibá;
Olibarito más esgrasasiaíto
No lo hay ni lo habrá.

I went out to the olive grove
To cry out my griefs;
Such a crummy little grove of trees
Never was or will be.

– Gypsy song

Main Train Station

You can wait here a long time.
—Main train station saying

It begins and ends with the main train station. You can go anywhere from the main train station, but you always come back. There is no way except the way through the main train station. It is large and dirty and grey. It smells of diesel fuel and cigarettes. The air through the skylights is grey. People run in the main train station. People sit in the main train station. People eat wurst and drink beer, read the newspapers, listen to the loudspeaker in the main train station. In winter the main train station is cold. In summer it is hot. People get on trains, people get off trains. People open the train windows and stick their heads out. People wave goodbye from the platforms.

The whole world is served by the main train station. Out of the main train station the cold steel tracks snake past warehouses and apartment buildings, over the rivers and roads, of a single giant city. The tracks coil back on themselves and return to the main train station.

There is only one city, and only one train station.

That's what you leave from, and that's what you go back to. The journey in between, the framed pictures snapping by—fields, cows, trees—is just a turn, half a turn, of the main train station track. Whether your trip lasts an hour or a week, you'll soon be back. A rush of noise, as though the window flew open (but it hasn't): another train shoots by. Faces, shuttered compartments, more faces. They're on their way back, too, and you'll see them again, but you won't know them at all, in the main train station.

Head of the President
(Five True Tales)

This café was on the somber side—badly lit, full of heavy furniture. The friends were telling stories. We were six in all. I was the only woman.

Botho said, "Head of the President."

"One day many years ago," Tom began, "my brother was walking in the Venezuelan jungle."

"How did your brother happen to be in the Venezuelan jungle?" asked Philip, though we all knew how.

"He was in the Peace Corps and had just built two hundred and fifty-one portable latrines out of cement and bamboo. He was on his way from the village that wanted the latrines to the village that didn't want them. He came around a bend in the trail and there was the head of the President in a Surinam cherry bush."

"Just the head?"

"It had been cut off from the body," Tom said.

"President of what?"

"President of Venezuela."

"And what was the head doing in the Surinam cherry bush?"

"It seems there was a coup in the capital. The young lieutenants kidnapped the President and took him into the countryside. Then they executed him."

"And threw away the head."

"So it seems."

"It was luck, fate," Jan said, "that your brother was walking on the trail that very day?"

"Yes, it was."

"What did he do with the head?"

"He put it in his backpack and took it to the village that didn't want the latrines. The matter was reported to the proper authorities."

Pleased sighs. Then Jan cleared his throat to a rustle of expectation. "Son of the Pope," someone whispered. Our second favorite story.

"Ninety years ago was war on another continent," Jan said heavily. "Which one doesn't matter. Scene is Polish front. Italians . . ."

"You said the continent didn't matter," —— broke in.

"*War* doesn't matter. It was Polish front." We all knew how patriotic Jan was. "Italians set to withdraw. Situation critical. Monsignor is sent from Vatican to meet with troops. Poles know, once this monsignor leaves again for Rome, Italian army goes with him. Generals confer. Beautiful Polish countess is sent for, situation explained. Night before Monsignor's departure, she comes to his door at little inn. Monsignor stays. Italian army stays. Poles jubilant.

Nine months later," Jan clasped his hands together held both arms away from his sides, and rocked them back and forth, "a smiling boy." He paused. "Today in Paris lives son of the Pope. Very old man now, of course."

A short silence fell. We were all mentally reviewing the repertoire.

"King of the Cats," Botho suggested, even though it was bad form to nominate your own story.

Jan made a motion of disgust. "Not that one! I am sick of hearing that one."

"It's a wonderful story," Philip said carefully, "But we have heard it many times, and as recently as last week."

Botho turned red. "In that case," he said lightly, "let it be your story."

Philip cleared his throat. One felt he'd been waiting for this. "Here comes a brand new story," he said. "And a brand new theme. Though it happened some time ago."

Bravo, Philip.

"I have an American friend, a professor of archaeology. Many years ago, when it was still a novelty, he purchased a word processor to write his life's work, a study of Plains Indian prehistory. He was called to an anthropological congress in Washington and brought, on floppy disks—"

"Floppy disks!" someone exclaimed.

"On floppy disks," Philip repeated, "the only

copy of his finished book. He had some free time. He decided to visit the Native American exhibit at the Smithsonian. My friend was especially taken with an enormous hunk of copper lodestone, part of a display on prehistoric metallurgy. This giant rock filled almost a whole room. He put down his briefcase and walked slowly around it, touching the places where the Sioux had chipped off pieces for a thousand years. Then he read the display card. With rising horror he realized this rock was a magnet—the biggest magnet in three states. And in the few moments he had circled the lodestone, it had reduced his life's work to a 30-second squawk."

Polite titters all around. But we felt restless, unfulfilled. The story was too new. It had no title, it wasn't properly broken in. Besides, Head of the President and Son of the Pope aroused expectations of the larger than life, not the merely anecdotal.

"Wife of the Worcestershire Sauce Company President was better," Tom said decisively.

Universal relief. This was the right sort of story, and we had not heard it for at least three weeks. Philip cleared his throat and began again.

"The wife of the Worcestershire Sauce company president was a lucky woman, but her husband was an unlucky man. Her husband owned a company whose product was the only thing people would leave in the kitchen cupboard when they moved. He was further unlucky in that one day on holiday he was run over by a truck."

"So how was his wife lucky?"

"She was lucky in that when her husband was run over by a truck she was able to sell his company and live off the proceeds with quite a nice young man in the Bahamas."

—— looked at me and winked. He was my special friend. I thought I knew what was coming next. —— was going to announce our wedding. But I was wrong. What he said was, "There were once six friends who got together every week to tell stories."

The others sat up. A *really* new story. "Every week they told each other stories," he said, "but there were only five real people. The sixth friend was Death. Death was waiting until they told all the stories so many times they couldn't think of any new ones."

Philip made a noise of protest, but —— waved him aside. "Any *good* new ones."

We all looked at each other, then at ——. I felt cold inside. Things had taken an unpleasant turn.

"What happens when all the tales are told?"

—— looked pleased. "Death tells the last tale. He eats you up."

"But Vicki hasn't told her story yet."

They looked at me. "She must tell a brand new story," —— said, "Not that old one she always tells."

My mouth opened, then shut. —— would not meet my eye.

"But this is ridiculous," Jan's voice shook slightly. "We are six people here."

"Look down at the table," —— said. "What do you see?"

We looked down. Five aperitif glasses, six people.

Tom said immediately, "One of us is a ghost. Not Death. A ghost."

Just then the lights went out.

How do you hide from a ghost in the dark?

I dropped to the floor and groped on hands and knees under the table. My arm brushed against a heavy material that smelled of mildew. A velvet curtain. I crawled under it into a brand new world. Here was a morning meadow. A dewy skeleton lay in the grass. Beside the skeleton stood a little girl. She said, "Follow me."

I followed her up the side of a barren mountain. It was a volcano. At the top I looked down into the crater, where clouds slid across a black lake the size of my thumbnail.

The little girl was gone. —— stood at my side.

"I'm the ghost," he said.

"I know." The great sadness in me was now complete.

He reached out as if to hug me but I knew he meant to push me over the edge. I stood firm and prayed to my grandmother's spirit. We wrestled. Even though —— was a strong and healthy man, he slipped in the loose dirt. I was able to pin him down.

"Please let me up," —— said. "If my whole body touches the ground, I'll die." Our heads were close and we looked deep into each other's eyes. His were flat as stones but I had loved him.

"If I let you up, you'll kill me."

"No, I won't," he lied.

I looked at him and did nothing. He made a small noise like escaping air. Under my hands the well-loved body sank. It withered along the hard contours of the ground. Then its shape shifted and it came to life again, an old man first, then a baby wiggling in my arms. Proudly I lifted him high, my own dear son. From far below rose the sound of voices. It was an outdoor café, where all my friends sat under red and blue umbrellas and the conversation showed signs of heating up again.

Draculess

Number One
Sweeping across the land in her glossy cloak of orange and black rooster feathers, seeking and not finding, what have I unleashed? My own personal vampire Draculess, Mistress of the Gods!

Underwater she's altogether neutral—a gentle, plump, benign creature. Breaking surface the first time, she grows a foot and drops a stone. Daylight bruises her pale skin. Her hungry eyes sink in their sockets. Yellow fangs sprout from her jaws.

She has a few abortive onshore adventures, about which I soon get an earful. It's my Draculess's one endearing quality that even now she's not as fearsome as she looks. An inept hunter, she hurls herself on predators far more advanced than she and so they vanquish her instead of the other way around. Mistress but no mistress, just a slave.

Back to the seashore, tail feathers drooping.

No, no, I say, this won't do. Is it the acts of predation I can't stand or just her incompetence?

I order her back down under. On the sea bottom a team of surgeons performs a life-saving operation. Through a neat incision in her side they remove an internal organ or two swollen with puss and bile, along with a few alien objects—broken pocket mirror, bent fork, table knife, dirty dollar bills, detritus like you find in the stomach of a shark. Using dainty stitches, they sew her up good as new. But it's hard to tell if the surgery made a difference. As long as she's underwater, she's her old inoffensive self. The big test is resurfacing.

Which sure as birds sing in the spring she's bound to do.

Number Two
Okay, head out of the water, this time it's looking better. No purple skin, no disconcerting incisor growth, the eyes have a bit of sparkle. But wait, what's happening to her hair? From mousy brown it's curling Medusa style into electric red and yellow. Eye catching, yeah—but deeply unnatural.

She's stretching now, ever so sensuously, shaking out those bright frizzy locks. Less corseted, more natural and thus more powerful, she strides up the beach, vamping for that perfect *Vogue* shot. The hem of her matching red-and-yellow satin gown leaves a messy track in the sand as she disappears over the top of the dunes. I shiver. World, watch out.

Draculess II is gone a long time. A very long time. I wait on the beach. Should I be doing anything? Answer: no.

She'll be back, my Draculess.

Draculess III: The Makeover

Here she comes, transformed again, though not (to my knowledge) in the healing ocean. Jeans, a faded sweater—"sincere" clothes, uh oh. The hair is now a modest slicked-down coif tinted a discreet auburn. She walks right up with a frank and open smile. Shakes my hand, at least it's not a phony hug, and looks me in the eye. Still no funny teeth, but there's that otherworldly extra height to deal with, a good seven feet now if I'm not mistaken.

Stands back, arms akimbo, voice warm and concerned: "How *are* you?"

Oh, I miss my funky Draculess. The naked, awkward one who let it all hang out. She's here, but it's going to take some digging to find her.

"How's your stomach, dear?"

Her brow furrows ever so slightly.

"I'll be happy if you're not swallowing flatware anymore. So uncomfortable."

Flatware, see? Not silverware. Not forks and knives. I'm aiming at the new one's level.

A cold, hard stare over my shoulder, then she turns away. In the language she's learned, this is the code for squelching impudence. She marches off, sand squeaking under her expensive loafers. The giant head bobs over the next dune, vanishes.

She'll be back, my Draculess.

Draculess Meets the Wolfman

In the end I go after her. If she's off having fun, why shouldn't I?

I walk and I walk and by the time night is falling I wind up in a great city. Standing on a busy street corner among the crowds, taxis, buses, noise—what to do?

Over the masses of heads I spot the distinctive cap of dark red hair, bobbing down Fifth Avenue. My dear creature wears a suit so simple it takes my breath away. I push through the throng to her side.

My Draculess gives me a knowing look but says nothing. Without slowing down, she heads for the arched entrance of a pearl-grey ziggurat whose iridescent pinnacle pricks the pink sky above us. Barely able to keep up, I follow her into the building. A uniformed doorman waves us through to the elevators.

Up, up we ride in a shiny gold chamber. Not a word passes between us, though many times I find myself about to speak. At the 101st floor the doors part. We walk into a penthouse. City lights and sunset catch fire in full-length windows. Blinded by the splendor, at first I don't see the man standing by the cocktail cabinet, the man my Draculess is embracing even as she towers over him. I say man, but above the impeccable dark suit sits a shaggy grey head all fur, teeth, lolling tongue.

They greet each other not with words but whimpers, growls, the occasional short bark, all very jolly, and suddenly I relax. It feels okay, I can scarcely say why.

I never imagined my Draculess mating. After a minute or two I foresee some problems. One, she's no longer under my control. I won't be able to send her underwater any time I feel like it. Two, what about me?

"You'll come with us," D. says. It's not a question.

Now this does not feel okay. Let her go? Fine, good riddance. But I'm not *her* creature. That's not what this is about.

"You've grown up and found a fine fellow," I tell her. "That's all I ever wanted for you." Not quite true, but it *is* a nice outcome. Better, I admit, than the uses I had meant to put her to. "I'm going home now."

Draculess and her lover whirl to face me, teeth bared. Hers are yellow tusks again, turned against me for the first time. They don't need to say a thing to tell me the answer is no.

When I sprint for the door, they rush me.

Big-Headed Boy
I'm locked up in a large cage on wheels next to the vanity dresser in an empty servant's bedroom.

I've turned into a boy child with a very large head.

They feed me on expensive bits of raw meat and

puréed vegetables in fancy shapes with little squiggles on top, presented on big china plates with linen napkins. I hate it because I'm seven years old and I know exactly what I want. I want a hamburger. I want to get back to the beach.

I've begged Draculess to let me go, but she says we can't be separated now or all her plans will fail. She and the Wolfman are presently engaged in getting more and more and more and more. As soon as they get just a little more than that, we will all go back to the beach.

I know this is nonsense, there's always more after the little more. Meanwhile I'm changing. For the worse. My head's getting bigger. Even though I am only seven years old, it looks like an old man's head, all watery eyes, chin whiskers, wattles. Down below, my little boy's penis grows ever tinier and more retracted.

Every night I have to listen to those two animals mating in the master bedroom. The howling and the grunting, it's enough to make you sick.

One morning I wait while Draculess unlatches my cage door, a ghastly salad of bitter greens and thistles in her hand. In a single movement I snatch the china plate and rap it on her head, hard.

She reels back in a shower of radicchio, clutching her bleeding forehead. I push past her out of the cage and bean her from behind with a heavy cut-glass perfume bottle from the vanity. She sags to her knees. I can't bear to hit her any more, not my own little Draculess, so I tie her hands behind her with nylon stockings (the vanity again), gag her, and stuff her into the cage on wheels.

In the art deco bathroom I fill up the tub with water and sink all the way under. Sure enough, the big head shrinks, goodbye penis. I climb out and look in the mirror.

Me again, more or less. I'm not seven years old. I don't need to go back under. But Draculess does.

How to get her home? I peek out the bedroom door. The lights are off in the hall. I crawl to the edge of the stairs and look over. The Wolfman sits in his beautiful brown leather armchair reading the *Times.* Smoke curls out of a pipe lying in the ashtray. I tiptoe down the hall to the master bedroom and snatch four long leather belts from a rack in a walk-in closet big as a barn.

Belts looped over my shoulder, I creep down the stairs and sneak up behind the armchair. Will those furry ears quiver, marking my step? Will that keen nose twitch with my human scent? The Wolfman reads on. Holding one belt high, I rise from behind the chair, fling the belt over his body with a whoop and cinch it tight. He howls in outrage, snapping at me with his big teeth. I do the same with the next belt, and the next, until he is well and truly buckled into his chair.

From the phone next to the chair I call a rental

company and order a truck. Then I go back upstairs, where Draculess writhes in the cage, making it shake with her fury. I cover the cage with the fancy flowered duvet from the bed, bump it downstairs, wheel it past her thrashing Wolfman to the door, the corridor, the service elevator, and the lobby.

The rent-a-truck waits at the curb.

Draculess: The Homecoming

I park my caged creature brazenly on the beach. I'm confident she didn't reveal her humble origins to the Wolfman and time proves my hunch correct. He never shows up.

But more needs to be done. I hire a crane. With a heavy heart—anticipating hissing flesh, decomposition, I don't know what—I lower the cage into the ocean. As it dips below the surface, Draculess puts up a ridiculous fuss. I turn my head away. The water closes over the cage.

I snorkel out for a look. There she sits on the sandy sea bottom, snarling through the bars.

Untransformed.

Okay, I can still get back to myself, but my Draculess can't. Her process is no longer reversible. Now what?

I haul her back up on the beach. I hate keeping her in the cage, but I can't risk letting her out. This time she's not depressed, she's furious. At me. There's murder in her pale eyes. Were our roles reversed, I wouldn't be getting fed radicchio, not this time.

All the same, as the weeks drag by, the desire grows in me to let her go. I'm not having as much fun back on the beach as I thought I would, not in the company of this unhappy creature pining for her Wolfman.

One night when the full moon rides high over the ocean, I find myself thinking: What does that moon look like over the city? I walk over to the cage where Draculess stands silent.

Trembling—for all that I love her, I can never forget what she is—I unlatch the door and open it.

In one dreadful movement she's out and on me, fangs breaking the skin on my neck. Then she stops. Steps back, wiping her bloody chin. Looks at me once with those pale intelligent eyes. Turning, flies off in the wind, back to the great city.

Spared, for now. I peer into the darkness she once occupied, the emptiness she left.

You'll be back, my Draculess.

Loglines*
(A Love Story)

A lawyer advises a young woman with money problems.
A young woman seeks security with an older man.
A womanizing lawyer falls for his sultry client.
A woman marries despite doubts about her husband-to-be.
A lawyer falls under the spell of his wife's cousin.
Marriage slowly erodes a sheltered woman's resolve.
An unhappy couple's pent-up frustrations surface.
A drifter awakens desire in a lawyer's neglected wife.
A woman plots to murder her philandering husband and a drifter takes the rap.
A wealthy widow seeks a new life after her husband's sudden death.
An artist pursues his dream woman and marries her.
A jealous ghost haunts the home of an artist and his wife.
A woman seeks a man to house her former husband's spirit.
An artist fears he is losing his wife to a satanic cult.
A lawyer reincarnated as a drifter stumbles into his former wife's life.

---

* With apologies to TV Guide.

Rose Canyon Adventure

By the time they get to the little canyon young Mister and Missus are not speaking to each other. Why is unimportant. Darkness is falling, the tent must be pitched. Later, when they creep inside, still not speaking, a cold spring moon is up.

Sunrise finds them in a dry riverbed full of snakes and stones. Ridges and furrows, traces of ancient water passage, have carved up the ground underfoot. Among the trees on the high bank sits their little car. The bank is crumbled where they climbed down the night before.

They're both awake and up. Mister walks over to a rock to inspect the area. Missus combs her hair.

Missus breaks a twelve-hour silence. "What is this place, anyway?"

"It must have rained up in the mountains," Mister remarks. "Look at those clouds."

The clouds at the top of the mountains are an ugly shade of purple. They look punctured, like old flat tires.

"But it's not going to rain here."

"No."

"I'm hungry."

Mister says, "I'll make a fire." Hitching up his pants, he wanders off to collect wood.

Missus gets out the pots and arranges them listlessly on the rocks.

Mister starts a fire.

The water boils busily over the fire as water has done these millions of years.

"Hand me your cup," Missus demands.

Mister clutches his cup tighter. "I don't want coffee. I'm going to put my cereal in this."

"I wasn't going to give you coffee. I was going to put cereal in it."

"You don't know how much I want."

"No, I don't. I surely don't." Missus gets up and kicks over the pot of water in the fire. Then she throws the spoon as far as she can down the dry riverbed.

Mister gets up and walks over to Missus. He grabs her by the ponytail and raises his hand as if to slap her. Missus raises her hand back. Mister lowers his hand and lets go her ponytail.

They sit down.

Mister sits on a five hundred thousand year old rock, Missus on a three hundred thousand year old one.

Mister whistles a few bars of something or other.

Missus says nothing.

"I'm going to pee now. Want to come hold my dick?"

Missus looks away. Ten yards down from them a snake slides under an overhanging ledge. (In alarm? Do snakes hear?)

When Mister returns, he takes a knife out of his pocket, opens the blade, and whittles at a dry branch.

High up in the mountains, at the source, a swollen gusset of water rises, bursts, and descends its old highway, sweeping up and swallowing every stick and bone in its path. Ancient sandstone fissures smile as the wall of water melts them into memory.

The branch breaks in two. Mister whittles the piece left in his hand.

The flash flood drowns seventeen king snakes, one rattler, two or three grey squirrels, a crippled deer, and that is not even counting the myriad insects, lizards, toads, all God's forgotten creatures who surrender their spark silently at the flood's demand. Caught in the branches, clumped pine needles, dissolved dirt and sandstone, they rush down toward the Rose Canyon bottleneck buoyed on the faster-moving top level of water.

Missus gets up heavily.

"Well," she says.

Mister looks over.

Sierra flash floods often build to crisis only to vanish at once, sucked swiftly into the earth's thirsty pores as soon as they reach the Central Valley. The flood pouring through the parched throat of Rose Canyon on this spring morning does not. This flood dumps its heavy cargo into a stream that sends it to the Eel, and the Eel sweeps it down and across, closer, closer, until nothing can stop its pell-mell race— not log jams, dikes, dams, not anything at all—to melt in the open sea.

One Million B.C.
(The Prehistory of Love)

There was a tiny herd of humans who lived in cave mouths on a cliff face deep in a fissure in the surface of the Plain. A man and a woman belonged to the herd. They picked each other the way you were supposed to. They mated. They sacrificed big lizards to the Spirits for kids to raise. Nothing happened. Time passed, and they felt restless. Then the man got an idea. He wanted to leave the herd and go looking for the "sea" that was supposed to lie at the end of the Plain. The woman didn't want to leave the herd. It's against the law to go on alone, she said. So the man's plan festered between them. Then he said to her one day he was going without her, because he had to. She didn't want to be left without him, so she agreed to go even though she didn't want to.

On a dark night under a crescent moon they ran away from the caves in the cliff, following the stream through the long narrow valley and up the steep mesa until they came out on the Plain. Dropping on their faces on the bare ground of the great dead Plain, they begged the Spirits to protect them. The man didn't tell the woman of his sure knowledge they would be killed by wild things long before they could reach the "sea." He needed to try to do it, that was all. He felt strong and daring under the stars.

The woman didn't complain, even though she was scared down to her bones. She had made up her mind to follow him. The feeling between them was wrong, but that didn't seem to matter. The woman thought: At least we're still together. The man thought: The herd will always remember me.

They walked over the dark Plain until the horizon glowed red. Bending their heads, they waded into the light of the rising sun. The Plain was wide as two continents, full of brush, bones, and sand. No rivers cut through, only pools and puny trickling streams. Raw young volcanoes broke its surface like boils.

Above them a great big bird with leather wings wide as two humans made a sad, dry noise like a cough, circled once and flew away.

The man and the woman walked until they stood at the shore of a huge shallow lake of salt water, all milky white and still. The caked salt deposits had worn giant cracks in the shore under their feet. They sat down on the cracked ground. They were tired and thirsty and they couldn't drink this water.

For the first time, the woman spoke up. "I wish I hadn't come. I wish I'd stayed with the herd."

"You didn't have to come."

"You're my mate. I had to."

This made the man think a bit. "You should have thought harder before you took my lizard skins," he said finally. "If you liked me more than the rest of our herd, you'd be glad to be here now."

"I like you, but I don't like this trip. This trip makes no sense, as far as I'm concerned."

"I can't help that," said the man. "You decided to come along. If it was me in your place, I wouldn't have come. I would've stayed true to my own heart, just like I'm doing now."

There was a silence. Then the woman, who felt degraded by these words, said, "There was another man of our herd before you. I liked him so much!" She named the man. "He wouldn't have me. The first time I said yes to you, I didn't like you. I still wanted that other man. But I came to like you. Now that I do, you don't like me."

The man didn't say a word back. He looked at the mountains. Inside he was hurt and shamed. He made up his mind not to speak to the woman again until they got to the end of their trip, to get even with her.

So they walked in stubborn silence. They came to little hills just as barren and stubbly as the Plain itself, but harder to walk on. They came to high hills and deep shadowy valleys like the one their herd lived in, only narrower and steeper. The man was dejected. So far there was no game and no water. But the woman began to feel strangely happy. She hummed to herself, walked fast, even got the man to start talking again. She didn't know why she was happy, but to her the trip wasn't a bad thing anymore.

Then there was a narrow gorge, a dark place with a pool of water hidden under an overhanging rock and a jumble of huge boulders blocking the other end. The water in the pool was clear and very cold. The man shivered in the thin air. He felt all heavy inside. But the woman, who had been getting more and more excited, said, "Come on! We're almost there!"

For the first time she led the way. She climbed up the spill of giant rocks that blocked the end of the gorge. Her feet stumbled in the ragged skin covers she had made when the stone underfoot had gotten too cold to walk on. She climbed furiously. Each rock, each handhold was like something from before, from the beginning.

Then she knew what was happening. She must be getting close to her own Spirit home. Back on the Plain, the herd believed that Spirits ruled everything. The men had talked a lot about the problem of where their souls came from. They tried to find this place again by returning to the land of the Spirits in dreams and trances. Sitting with the other women in the shadows outside the ring of men around the special fire, the woman had listened to each man talk about what he had seen on his soul trip.

Now, struggling to the top of the big rockslide, the woman could see that most of the men had been lying about their soul trips just to look good; only a few had really seen anything. But nobody in the herd, not even the ones with the true sight, had let on that they'd known the difference. Maybe that was because they, unlike her, had to go back to their life in the herd when their visit was over with. But she was getting to her soul place in her own body, with no herd to take her back when it was over. Yes, her soul hadn't been too keen about this trip at first. But when it was close enough to pick up the scent, it had homed in like a hunter.

The woman raised her head over the last rock. There was a big scooped-out valley with a shiny lake, slightly sunken, set right in the middle like a great big eye. Gentle green plant shoots, soft but thinly spaced like baby hair, grew all around the lake. Trapped in its surface was the upside-down Spirit of the giant white ghost peak that loomed over the valley.

She stood up and walked into the valley.

Meanwhile the man was still trying to get up the rocks. His energy was almost gone. When he finally pulled himself over the top, the very sight of the white peak in the lake was such a strong Spirit that he lost his grip and tumbled back down the slope. With shaking hands he hoisted himself back. When he looked over the top this time, he kept his eyes carefully away from the lake and the mountain.

The woman was nowhere to be seen. To the left of the lake was a cluster of giant pale rocks high as five humans. The man thought he saw something move behind them. It might be the woman, but he was not going to try to find out. He was not going to step off the rocks to set his feet down in this valley, now or ever. It was a terrible place. And just as he had this thought, his shoulders slumped and he fell into a kind of trance.

It was late afternoon and bitter cold when he woke up. The sun slanted straight into the bowl of the valley, making it burn with light. The woman was standing in front of him. She had come up without a sound.

She was so changed he almost didn't know her. Her body was covered up in a bulky robe of silver skins. Carved wooden sticks and woven strips of cloth stuck out of her hair. Pieces of shiny flat rock hung from her ears. Five heavy bracelets clattered on her left wrist. And when she spoke—what a difference!

"I'm staying here with the old woman," she said. "You have to go."

Some way behind her in the valley the man could make out a squat, terrifying human form; he wasn't brave enough to look more closely. The woman was handing him some packets of salted meat and a worn fuzzy brown beast skin. Without saying another word—but with a quick look over her shoulder at him that punched his heart—she turned around and walked back into the valley.

The force of the old female Spirit behind her was so strong the man couldn't say a word back. He couldn't make a move to stop the woman. He was so scared that he put on the coat, slung the packets in a bundle over his shoulder, and started back down the rockslide. He didn't turn around to look at the two figures, one tall and one short, moving toward the white rocks beside the lake.

The trip down the rockslide and through the gorge was quick and easy; the Spirit that had stopped the man from getting in got him out fast. By nightfall he was a long, long way from the valley where the woman was. After that came lots of hard days of walking. The fear that took him over when the Spirit pushed at him went away slowly. Grief and confusion over losing the woman took its place. Then he tried to get back to the way he felt about going to find the "sea." He had wanted to find the sea for so long. Now the wanting wasn't there anymore. He was empty inside. But there was nothing to do but go on. If the woman wasn't with him, she wasn't with him—it couldn't be helped.

He passed other white peaks, walking through open passes and meadows across the mountains. None of them was a Spirit like the one in the valley lake. The hills got smaller and lower, the sky got bigger, the ground dried up. The man's soul pushed him faster and faster. One day he stood on a cliff. Beyond it was a shimmer like the Spirit water his herd had known on their Plain. But the shimmer reached out to the farthest point his eyes could follow. It was the sea.

There was a tribe of humans living in driftwood huts on a sand flat right by the sea. They grew stalks in fields next to their huts and even floated dead hollow trees on the surface of the water to hunt sea beasts. They made wonderful tools and always had plenty to eat.

Into this tribe the man was taken. He learned their words and their way of hunting the best he could. He built a hut and took a woman. With her he had three red-headed kids whose ways caught him up in a net of daily worries and love. Now that he was here, he found he did not much care about the sea. It was hard to switch hunting skills, and the rocking dead trees on the water made him sick. To have come this far, he thought, was plenty. So he had to take his place as the Stranger, a somewhat backward member of the tribe.

Sometimes he could hardly even remember what had set him off on his big trip from the Plain. So he made up a little ditty about his adventure to sing to the men of his new tribe. They were willing to believe but weren't too interested. They looked to the sea, not to the land behind them. A long time back, people of their tribe had come over the mountains from the Plain to settle here. Who wanted to hear about that ugly place from the past? Besides, it was a well-known fact that the Plain was inhabited by devil ghosts. The man himself had been put through a highly painful ordeal just to prove he was a human, not a Spirit.

He had almost forgotten his woman from the Plain when she came to him one night in a dream. In the dream she was a grey fox. The fox sat on the rocks at the mouth of the valley of the white peak. The woman's eyes, full of love and longing, looked out of the fox's head. No wind ruffled the fur on her back or the blades of grass around her; it was all very still. Every bit of the picture was alive, burning into the man's heart.

When he woke up, his life with his new wife and their kids in the little hut by the sea became the dream. The only real thing was the grey fox in the valley. A big feeling of nothing came over him. He couldn't do his daily rounds. He sat inside the hut. He wouldn't come out. He refused to talk or eat.

The tribe saw that their Stranger had been taken over by Spirits from his old life, over which the magic of their tribe had no authority. The elders said that the Stranger had to be taken back to the top of the trail from the mountains where he had first been found. All limp and quiet, the man was carried by litter into the foothills and dumped at the bottom of the cliff he had first seen the sea from. The magic chief tore off the man's bracelets and nose ring, the signs of his belonging to their tribe. They poured urine over his head to cancel out the anointment from his initiation. Then the magic chief and the litter carriers left as fast as they could down the trail.

The man sat still at the foot of the cliff. He was only a thing that took up space, blocking the wind. Then the fox was sitting on the ground in front of him, licking the ruff of fur around its neck with a quivering pink tongue. The man's eyes opened wide. It was the woman in her silver robe.

For a while he just looked at her, even though rain was falling lightly on their heads. "Why did you leave me?" The minute he asked it, the question seemed useless.

The woman didn't answer right away. Then she said, "The old woman is a big priestess. She wanted to teach me the things she knew about. As soon as you and I got in the mountains, I could hear her calling me. But it was all settled long before that. When we were still with the flock on the Plain, the old woman took over your heart and made you want to go look for the sea. That way, you could bring me to her."

"She gave me my plan to get to the sea?" The

man was deeply shocked.

"The old woman has been teaching me her Spirit secrets," the woman went on. "She hasn't said for sure, but I think I'm supposed to take her place when she gets too old to do her daily rounds. I broke my promise never to leave the valley by coming here. I gave the old woman something to make her sleep for three days. I wouldn't have come, except I saw you in a dream. I couldn't stop thinking about you."

"I had a dream, too," the man said bitterly. It made him sick to think of how he'd been pushed around by Spirit forces, all the time thinking he was cutting a brave new path all by himself. As for his stupid and futile love for the woman, what Spirit plan was behind that? What selfish goal of the Spirits was he blindly carrying out now? He felt his heart harden against this tangle of invisible plots.

But oh, he was caught! He couldn't stop his eyes from pleading with the woman. He said, "Won't you come with me now?"

The woman jumped away from his stare. The air around her rippled, she became a hazy blend of fox and woman. "Back on the Plain," she said, "you told me I should be true to my heart the way you were. I still don't exactly know what that is. Being away from you was a lot harder than I thought it would be. But I wanted to learn the old woman's secrets. I want to go back and be a big priestess. Don't try to talk me out of it."

By now she was all fox, standing up on her four legs. The man looked at her without saying a word back. Then she gave a quick leap sideways into a thicket and dashed up the cliff.

After a while the man got up and started walking south under the cliffs, his heart full of painful feelings. To think of the woman at all was unbearable, so he didn't. What bothered him was thinking he'd been just a tame beast for the woman's Spirit in his great trip from the Plain. Where was his own Spirit to lead him now? Surely he had one. If it wasn't what he used to think it was, then it had to be something else. And if the woman had her valley—every time this thought crossed his mind, a terrible black hole opened inside him—if she had her valley, where was his Spirit home? He would have to start another trip to find it. But this time he could only go with no plan at all, just hoping this way the meaning would come out and his true Spirit would find him.

Meanwhile, returning by secret ways to the valley in the mountains, the woman had reached the rockpile in the gorge. Suddenly a strong force seemed to push against her, blocking her way. With a big effort she pulled herself to the top of the pile. Lifting her head over the edge, she gasped. Across the meadow, under the big pale rocks by the lake, the old woman faced her. The old woman's Spirit force was stopping the woman where she held onto the rocks. As hard as she tried, she couldn't get any farther into the valley. Next to the old woman was a young girl wearing a fur robe black as night. As she watched, helpless, the old woman and the girl turned and disappeared behind the rocks.

All night long, lying tired and sick at the bottom of the rockpile, the woman begged in her heart for the Spirit of the old woman to come to her. Nothing happened. The old woman was getting even with her for leaving the valley, she guessed. But it was worse knowing she'd lost the man and the valley both. Maybe it hadn't been a crime against her Spirit to leave the valley after all. Maybe her true crime against her Spirit had been not to go with the man when she had secretly wanted to. Or maybe, by breaking her promise and visiting the man, she was only following another one of the old woman's secret plans for her life? The woman felt very confused. Whatever the reason, now she had to live the rest of her life outside the valley with its mysteries forever closed to her.

When the hot morning light broke into the narrow gorge the next day, she knew what she wanted to do. She wanted to find the man.

Setting off at a headlong run, the woman found the valley magic clinging to her. As she came down from the mountains to the sea, she could no longer control her human shape. Sometimes she walked on two legs, sometimes on four; the fox came and went at will. But she kept on. She never stopped in one place for longer than it took to feed herself and sleep, always looking for that one who had been there before her or after her but never at the same time.

After missing him in village after village down the coast, the woman knew something was never going to let her close the gap—the man's Spirit, the old woman's, her own. But she couldn't stop, her Spirit pushed her on.

Meanwhile the man roamed tribeless along the coast. He stopped in villages to sing a little song about his life, how he and the woman had come from the Plain and what had happened to them. The villagers fed him but kept their distance. With all he'd gone through, the man already seemed half Spirit. And they saw what he couldn't, trailing behind him at every step: the ghost of the woman, and the lesser ghosts of his second woman and three kids. For these coastal tribes believed that failed matings leave powerful Spirits that pursue their human hosts until death.

With all their wanderings the man and the woman began to lose their bodies and after a while they became Spirits. Even then there was no rest; they had to keep trying to find human souls to move into and take over so they could keep their search going for each other. In time, they became very dangerous Spirits; that is what their love finally came to. Now, when the coastal tribes see one cloud chasing another at the same speed across the sky or two rocks frozen so they lean but never touch, they say, "It's the man and the woman!" And they touch a tree for protection, because it's not a good sign.

Halawa Valley Slide Show*

1. Down through the clouds, deep blue ocean turns to green where the coral reef breaks.
2. The island of Molokai.
3. Green cliffs drop to sandy beaches and deserted coves.
4. This is Halawa Valley.
5. Narrow in the mountains, wide at the shore.
6. And a small harbor at the mouth.
7. The Kahalewai family has their summer camp here.
8. They hunt wild pig and pick opihi, the saltwater limpet.
9. Mrs. Kahalewai is shelling opihi.
10. Mr. Kahalewai is having a beer.
11. Russell and big sister Armine watch their uncle Eli climb on the rocks under the cliffs.
12. Opihi picking can be dangerous.
13. Uncle has a full bag already.
14. Russell and Armine play in the surf with their cousins.
15. Watch out!
16. Ilio the dog gets in the swim.

---

* Narration to be read aloud with numbered slides.

17. Russell calls to Armine.
18. Let's go exploring!
19. Down the dirt road into Halawa Valley.
20. Past the abandoned church, past the empty houses.
21. No one has lived here in forty years.
22. Their great aunt Tutu Ann's bungalow.
23. Let's peek.
24. Russell, don't go in!
25. Look what I found.
26. A Sunday school diploma from long ago.
27. There is something behind the cardboard.
28. A photo of Auntie Tutu Ann as a young girl.
29. Oh, so pretty!
30. Come, don't hang around.
31. For they know Auntie Tutu Ann's grave is in the back yard.
32. Close the gate behind you.
33. The diploma left on the porch steps.
34. Now Russell and Armine are at the end of the road.
35. The old trail follows the stream back into the mountains.
36. Old terrace walls where Russell's ancestors cultivated the taro plant.
37. Ilio chases a mongoose.
38. A wild orchid for Armine's hair.
39. Russell teases Armine.
40. I saw you here with Kaipo.

41. Shut up, silly boy.
42. Patches of sun and shadow under the java plum trees.
43. Look, soft pili grass to sit in.
44. From here you can see down the whole valley to the ocean.
45. There is Moa Ula waterfall.
46. And this is Makaelele.
47. Mountain apples, ripe and tasty.
48. What a pleasure to sit and eat.
49. The beauty of the afternoon.
50. A big black dog attacks!
51. But it is only a dream.
52. Armine was asleep.
53. Now there are long shadows everywhere.
54. Time to go back to the beach.
55. Ilio, go slow!
56. Let's take a different trail.
57. The darkness of the forest.
58. Like a giant spider web, the tangled roots of the hau tree.
59. Armine is frightened.
60. Pick a ti leaf for protection.
61. What's that big pile of lava rocks around the bend?
62. The ruin of a heiau.
63. Here their forefathers worshipped the god of sharks.
64. Russell trips over a root.

65. His leg is hurt.
66. And the shadow across his face.
67. Is it an accident?
68. Armine has a thought.
69. Her brother is marked for an early death.
70. Past the heiau, into the sunshine!
71. See the family waving from the beach.
72. Papa has made a toy boat for Russell.
73. How come you limping, son?
74. Russell and his boat darken the mouth of the stream.
75. Armine helps her mother cook the rice.
76. Time for dinner, everyone!
77. There is always plenty to eat.
78. And coconut haupia for dessert.
79. The glow of a brilliant sunset.
80. The Kahalewai family watches from the beach.
81. Gentle surf laps the shore.
82. Armine sits deep in thought.
83. What of the future?
84. And her brother so silent.
85. Her family is talking and laughing.
86. And it is already dark.
87. Then you must say goodbye to unhappy thoughts.
88. Tonight all will lie down well fed and at peace.

Four Oahu Tales

Old Woman and the Cat
Neighbor family fumigates their home for island termites. Big gaily striped tent goes over the house, family stays overnight in a Waikiki hotel. Move back to their immaculate ranch house all free of pests for another five years, something is wrong. Ugly sweet odor rises from the floors and hangs in the air, clings to Daughter's pretty clothes in her closet. Finally someone says: "Dead animal under the house," and he is right. Look under the porch, what a smell! Stray cat hid there when the tent went over the house. Now he is dead and rotting.

    No one wants to go get that cat under the house, not after a week. Too much stink, disgusting. Then someone brings old wrinkled four-foot grandmother. Mama-san looks under the porch, grunts, crawls in with kerchief over her face and mango picker bag in her hand. Everybody waits. Soon she comes backing out on hands and knees. Oho, they think. But Mama-san only says, "You bring me one shovel and bucket. All his skin come off in one piece when I lift it." Daughter and friends squeal. Daddy brings the bucket and shovel. Mama-san crawls under the house again. Sound of shovel hitting rim of pail. When Mama-san comes out from under the house this time, everybody backs off.

"Here," she said to her son. "You go bury." "Yes, Mama," says Daddy with a nervous laugh. He holds the bucket with one hand and his nose with the other. Daughter asks, "What kind of cat, Grandma?" but Mama-san declines to answer.

The Pig That Knew the Trick

Out in the country, blonde young John finds a lost baby pig, takes it back to blonde Susan to raise in the tin-roof shack. They feed garbage to the little black pig and keep him tied to the mango tree out front. That pig grows and grows till he is high as Susan's waist. He weighs 500 lbs. and stands like a statue in the dust under the mango tree. Fruit flies boil around him like shoals of fish. But Susan taught him a trick when he was little and he still can do it. She reaches down and scratches his hairy gray belly. That is the signal. Grunting and wheezing, the pig drops to his knees and rolls over like a steamboat capsizing. Four horn hooves hang in the air. The cloud of fruit flies regroups over his new position. Slowly the great pig rubs his back in the dead leaves and smashed mangoes. The air is full of country noises. Imprisoned in the giant head, the little pig eyes look up.

The Dog That Hung Himself

Peanuts, uptightest dog in Niu Valley. His owners keep him leashed inside a cage in the chainwire-fenced back yard. Peanuts throws himself in a frenzy against the side of the cage whenever a face appears in the kitchen window fifteen feet away. Tries to scale the chain link wall in sheer excitement till the leash yanks him back and he falls to the ground in choking fits. "How come your dog so *nervous?*" neighbors say to the Chinns. "How come you no pet him, take him for walk?"

The Chinns don't like other people butting into their business. They go on just like always. When they were little, Peanuts was Brother and Sister's beloved pet. But no more. Brother and Sister are in high school, their friends come over to play music. They don't want Peanuts, they put him in the cage because he's a nuisance. Sometimes Sister comes to coo baby talk through the wire to the little dog. When he gets too excited, she slaps him and leaves.

All day and all night Peanut screams like a human. Teenage girl across the street crawls through the fence one night and unhooks the gate to let Peanuts get away from the Chinns. But Peanuts won't go. Body shaking all over, he crawls to the kitchen door to cry and moan. Peanuts wants love, not freedom.

Other neighbors have different ideas. Haole schoolteacher wants to call the SPCA, Hawaiian telephone linesman wants to poison his food, surfers want to kidnap him and take him to the North Shore. In the end nobody has to do anything. Brother and Sister go out in the back yard one morning, find Peanuts dangling from his leash on the side of the cage. (Leash caught on the chain links during one of his frenzied charges.) His swollen tongue hangs out, his little eyes bulge. Doo-doo lies all over the ground and in his bowl. Disgusting.

Faceless Woman and the Dog-Faced Man
You get in a taxi in Waikiki—says Kaipo—you tell the driver take you home. But he don't go that way, he take you to the back of Manoa Valley to the graveyard. Then he turn around in the seat and you see under the little hat he got the face of a white dog. And he smile at you with his big yellow teeth, 'cause he going to tear your heart right out of your living body.

You a girl, you go da movies, you go Waialae Drive-In in Kaimuki, watch out. You walk in the women's room top of the hill, it's over a burial ground. You see an old Chinese lady standing at the mirror with a long Chinese dress slit up the side and gray hair in a bun. That's what you see from the back. She just standing there. Then you look in the mirror and you see the lady got no face. You see her one time, she casts a spell on you forever. And that's no lie. She don't have to tear your heart out to ruin your life for good.

Dead Lover

Ninety percent of fatal car accidents take place within one mile of the victim's residence.
—News report

George had lived with her about a year and a half when it happened. They had an arrangement; they weren't in love, they just shared sex and companionship. That was what George liked to say, at any rate. Well, she wasn't going to rock the boat. If saying that made George feel safe, she didn't care. He kept on coming home every night, that was what counted. He was hooked. So let him talk about his arrangement. One time he went on a trip and fell in love with a woman he met in a distant city. He wrote passionate letters to the woman and talked a lot about moving. Alarmed, she waited in silence. As the weeks and months passed, the letters dropped off and she knew he was going to stay put. It irked her to think that he could "love" someone far away and just have an arrangement with her, who shared his life with him, but she was afraid to take a stand and kick him out. It was hard to find someone new. She'd been alone for a long time before she met George and had almost given up. And George was good with

Davey, her little boy. She knew George didn't want to be like a husband and father, but that's what he was, living there with them, no matter what he said. In fact, everything that passed between them was a contradiction of what he said.

Once in a while, she got blazing mad that such a pale counterfeit of her dreams shared her bed and life. His topics of conversation, his little hobbies, were so rigid, so *George.* That was the price, of course. She paid it. She would not trade boredom for the other.

So the arrangement was six months old, then a year old, then more. And love or no, they merged into each other's rhythm. George was still fighting the current, of course. But his rants grew more sporadic as the hypnotic routine of their life deepened.

One morning, just after Davey caught the school bus and she was about to leave for work, she saw a long white ambulance with red lights flashing at the end of the street and a big truck crashed against a telephone pole. A neighbor beckoned her urgently. Two paramedics took her to the back of the ambulance. They lifted up a sheet and she saw George's bloody face. He had left the house five minutes before on his way to the corner Seven Eleven for some cigarettes. She rode down in the front seat of the ambulance to the coroner's office. George was the first dead person she had ever seen, and that was the start of the whole business.

George dead was different than George alive. For one thing, and it was no small thing, she now had complete control over him. Ten years before, when he was twenty-five, he had a serious quarrel with his parents and had broken off all communications with them. George had been so vague about his origins that she did not even know what state they lived in. He had been an only child, you could see that from the way he acted. So there was no one but her to see to the funeral arrangements. That meant she also had to sign the death certificate, close his bank account, notify the little welding company he worked for, and take over all the other duties of legally terminating his existence as a human being. Although she had not lived with him long enough to qualify for rights as a domestic partner, there was no one else to do the things that had to be done. George had not left a will, because he had nothing to bequeath and because he had not yet given up the idea that he was going to live forever. So the bank became the executor of his estate, such as it was. The Jeep Cherokee (not paid for), the checking account (modest), the tool kit, the video camera, a Star Wars memorabilia collection he'd held onto from boyhood. They took the account and the Jeep, gave her the rest.

George had some cronies, old drinking friends, whom she notified. Other than that, there was really no one. George had been a loner. In all the time he had lived at her house, he received little mail. In fact, that had been a difficulty when he started writing to the woman in the distant city. Her first letter to him had been returned "addressee unknown" and George told her the woman was sure she had intercepted it, but it was actually because the postal carrier didn't know he lived there.

The woman was a problem. George had not received any letters from her in a while, but what if a letter came now? Should she open it? George had not kept any of the woman's letters—afraid she would find them, she guessed, jealous of his privacy—but her name and address were in his address book. Should she write a note?

There was no funeral as such, and no services. She had him cremated, and his drinking buddies and her friends came over for a small wake. Davey helped serve the food. It was a somewhat subdued gathering because death was new to most of them. They were beginning to understand that if it could strike George, it could just as easily strike them.

How she herself felt she couldn't say. She had been too busy those first days taking charge of the end of George's life, picking up after him, so to speak, just as she had done when he was alive. When George's friends left the wake, she knew she would not see any of them again, because they were his friends and not hers. At that moment she felt a brief sharp pain.

The major duties were over the first week. By

the end of the month, the flow of legalities had diminished to nothing. Once George had officially died on paper, he ceased to be of interest to the world. The third week after his death she gathered up his clothes and few possessions from all over the house and packed them into three cardboard boxes to store in the garage. She did not know what else to do with them—the sizes were wrong for his friends and it was too soon, somehow, to call the Goodwill.

Six weeks after George's death she still felt the same as she had one heartbeat after looking into his single open starred eye in the back of the ambulance. He had left so little behind in friends, goods and affection that if it hadn't been for the three cardboard boxes in the garage, she would almost have wondered if he ever existed. He had been a ghost while he was still alive. By choice, of course. He had wanted to live free of entanglements. She always winced when he said that. She lived deep in the heart of the entanglement, in fact she *was* the entanglement as far as he was concerned. She couldn't imagine living any other way. If she died, there would be Davey, her parents and brother and sister, her friends and her ex-husband, and then her little house, her Toyota and picture albums and confirmation dress and everything else, and of course a will providing for the distribution of all these things. Of course, in the end it did not make any difference— that was the point. But she thought it was horrible in a way that George died with so little, living in his arrangement, not having anyone to grieve deeply for him, not even his own family, just because deep emotion had made him nervous in life. Entanglement. Hadn't he been in one all along, just by being alive?

She had not yet grieved for him, and she felt cheated. It meant that he had managed to set the limits on her affection as well as his own. In her whole way of handling his death, curiously, she had acted just like George. Except for the wake, which he wouldn't have bothered with, she did exactly what he would have done in that situation. She took care of things efficiently, philosophically, with a minimum of feeling. If she had treated him that way in life, she would have lost him. George craved emotionalism as much as he claimed to despise it. He could not endure cold women—or rather, he fell in love with them because they were cold and rejected him, but he could only live with an old-fashioned submissive woman like herself.

So the detached spirit that came over her when he died seemed new and exciting. It made her feel powerful and controlled, a sensation she had never had before. She began to radiate a certain stern authority that friends remarked on. In time she changed her job and took on a supervisory position at another business.

One morning six months after George's death, she was sweeping under the bed when a hard little object rolled out on the floor. It was a film container. She recognized it at once as part of George's marijuana kit. She was used to coming upon these relics of his at odd moments in unexpected places. It did not move her. She unscrewed the cap and sniffed. The grass was still fresh, she would smoke it tonight when one of the men she was seeing come over. She set it on the night table and forgot about it.

Later that day she chided herself for her cold-bloodedness, but in rather an abstract way. It only seemed heartless in principle—otherwise, she was indifferent. George had operated on principle, or maybe "opposition" was a better word. He constructed his set of beliefs so that they would be contrary to what anybody else believed. George couldn't bear having anyone share his opinions. Sometimes it got confusing, because there were other people who constructed their beliefs the same way, and when he reacted to them he ended up sounding rather conservative.

When she took out the dope that evening, her latest male friend remarked on how expertly she rolled the join—one handed, with precision and finesse, producing a tight, firm cigarette. She laughed and shrugged, it meant nothing to her. Later that evening she said, about someone's fractured romance, "Never mind, the bus leaves every five minutes." That startled her. Before, whenever George said, "The bus leaves every five minutes," she would bridle and assure herself inwardly that she didn't believe that nonsense. Now she was saying it. Did she believe it? She made a short review of her feelings and discovered, with a slight sense of alarm, that she did. It bothered her to think her whole sense of values could shift without her being aware of it.

The men she was seeing now were a different sort, for her. Instead of the tight-lipped, dogmatic, mechanically minded egotists she had once been drawn to—and that category included her ex as well as George—she now began to collect happy-go-lucky emotional types. One had even cried in front of her. Instead of hanging around her house watching television and waiting for her to get their supper, these men took her out dancing or escorted her and Davey to the zoo. They all knew how to cook. It was delightful and contemptible, she couldn't decide which. She was always breaking up with them and sending them away—no one of them could hold her attention very long. It was impossible for her to stick to the same man when a new opportunity was always around the bend.

She enrolled in a kickboxing class and Davey abandoned his Big Wheels for a watercolor set. It was a whole new life. Who was that domestic, bovine creature of long ago? She could no longer even remember what it had been only the year before.

But even as she plunged into one activity after another, an idea, a germ of something, was rising like a boil beneath the surface of her consciousness. What could it be? Something old but new, she sensed, out of the future and out of the past. One day it swelled unbearably and burst. She went out to the garage to the three cardboard boxes and cried in harsh, ugly hiccups. It was George! She loved George. She had always loved him, would always love him, no one else could ever replace what he had been to her. He was her true love, and he was dead. She thought of the bloody body wrapped in sheets and the pain was so horrible she started looking around the dark, damp interior of the garage for a knife to slit her throat with. She ripped open the boxes and buried her head in his flannel shirts, his jacket, baying like a hound dog. "It was you all along. You, you, you."

She lurched into the house and collapsed on her bed. After the first tumult passed, she began to think, slowly and clumsily. She was deeply in love with George, she realized. But the faint, dusty memory of their days together told her she had not loved him *then*. She loved him a little, of course, she needed him a lot, but it was no passionate romance, not even a companionship built out of deep respect—that was the trouble all along. When the pain subsided, she resumed her thoughts. Something was wrong. Why love him now? Why not then, when he was alive? That was just the kind of trick George always pulled on himself, like that whole business of the woman in the distant city he thought he loved so much.

Then she understood what had happened. She was not herself. She was George, and she was in love with George. But understanding did not alter the state of her feelings. Her sadness, her love, gripped her so strongly she could scarcely breathe. She was going to die.

For days she kept the house shut up, refusing to answer the telephone. Friends knocked on the door and she told them to go away. She called in sick at work and sent Davey across the state to his grandparents' house. She had to be alone to commune with herself—and George.

Images and fantasies floated across her brain, driving her to the edge of madness. George was a devil with pointed teeth, poised to suck her blood. George was a gentle Christ of infinite mercy who opened his arms to embrace her in loving tenderness. George was laughing, vividly alive, realer than real. He was crying, begging her not to abandon him, not to leave him in the cold, empty mortuary where the fire would burn his tender flesh to ashes, to nothing, to nothing beyond nothing.

"I won't! I won't! I promise I won't!" she shrieked. She beat the pillows, sprawling and kicking on the shambles of her bed. But it did no good. Each time he left her she passed through the agony of his death in its fullest, only to have him spring to life once more at the foot of her bed.

He wanted her to die with him, of course. He led

her to the pills, the car, the butcher knife and the bathtub, but each time she balked. Finally, poised one evening on the shore of a depressing bay while dirty grey wavelets lapped hungrily at her feet, she said, "No, George, this is enough." It was so exactly her old, patient voice that something lifted off her shoulders like a cloud. She used to say just those words to him when he proposed a money-making scheme that was more outlandish than usual or was urging her to try a new sexual position she knew would hurt her back. It always took a lot, in those days, to get her to come out and say it. When, pushed to her limit, she finally did, he would accept it and leave her in peace. And it happened now, because she used her old, lost voice. She got in her Ford Escort and drove home. It was over. She did not love George. She was not George. She was not exactly her old self, either. She had no idea what was going to happen next.

And what became of the real George, ash-George, the one who was struck by a truck and killed? He was now a great silence. Whether this silence lay at the center of her life or only lapped its edges—that she never knew.

Two Women

Mona and I changed from best of friends to worst of enemies because of a man.

I saw the woman I let into my confidence turn from a comrade into a Fury. Her betrayal provoked in me a hatred I never expected to experience.

My friend Mona and I were seekers. For what exactly, neither of us could say. We first met in a Gurdjieff study group. Exploring other spiritual disciplines together, we found we were perfect complements. Each made up for what the other lacked. Mona was more spontaneous, more warm and loving than I, but my impartial attitude guided her many times through perilous waters. Neither of us could hurdle the emotional barrier that kept us from becoming intimate with men, though we both excelled in brief encounters. It surprised me that Mona with her beauty and fun-loving nature should have just as much difficulty as I, who am not so traditionally feminine, in handling her love affairs.

We discussed the matter endlessly.

Baring our feelings of inferiority, we dissected each other's personality to see where the fatal flaw made its appearance. "There is something sad and heavy inside you that pushes men away," Mona told me. "You throw yourself at supermasculine men who torture and reject you," I counseled her. But it was too easy to dissolve in bitterness and place the blame squarely on men and their undeveloped emotional natures. When we gave in to this temptation, like children gorging themselves on cake, we could itemize the faults of every man we knew with a thoroughness of insight that bordered on genius.

Mona and I knew the dangers of this path. We knew that female narcissism is a closed circle. To break out meant exercising the highest form of forgiveness—so we tried to keep faith. All winter long, friendship sustained us.

At Easter I went away to visit my family. When I returned, Mona had news for me. While I was gone, she had met a man. Not any man, not in the least like her usual choice—the kind I called "cowboys"—but a special person, open and sensitive. "Reynaldo has feelings, like us," Mona explained. She knew I would like him very much. Of course, Reynaldo had heard all about me, too. When Mona introduced us at her house it was with the unspoken understanding that we were the two most important people in her life.

I liked Reynaldo—Rennie, he asked me to call him—right away, though I could not see the sexual attraction Mona felt for him. He was a small-boned Manila urbanite with jet black hair and shining brown eyes and an easy charm that welcomed you into his presence. But I sensed at once that he looked to Mona in subtle ways for support and approval. And she, smiling down at him like a big satisfied cat, would give it or not give it, according to her whim. Since between myself and Mona there had been nothing but harmonious confluence, I saw now for the first time the enormous power she wielded in emotional situations.

Rennie was a lady's man—so Mona informed me. At home in the subtle currents of female sensibility, he had racked up an impressive score as a lover. Though the reason for the breakup of so many affairs was unclear, a number of women in our city still carried the torch for Rennie. Some of them had even become close friends afterwards and were often seen together at public gatherings. None of this was displeasing to Mona, whom Rennie showered with presents and attention in a manner she had never known before. His deference made Mona feel she had the situation well under control. In fact, his dependence grew so quickly that Mona would retreat at times in a kind of sullen panic, which only served to incite him further.

Round and round they went. Months passed, yet the two of them did not seem to be coming closer together. Mona and I saw less of each other—we were no longer in the closest confidence—but I knew she was not succeeding in making a go of the thing with Rennie. There was the slightest hint of contempt in her voice when she mentioned his escapades, his enthusiasms. She did not love him, she said, or did not know if she did. His devotion she found claustrophobic. He was weak. She was tired of him.

In spite of myself I began to feel a certain sympathy for Rennie as underdog. Mona's constant criticism seemed petty and unfounded. I admired the free play of his emotions, though I also sensed the peculiar softness Mona found so disagreeable. I felt sorry for Rennie. This was the first time in all his string of conquests, I imagined, that he had experienced such a failure of confidence. I was rooting for him. I wanted him to break through the wall of Mona's icy disdain and win her for his own.

But while Mona struggled with Rennie, I lapsed back into the isolation and depression I had so painfully crawled out of during the winter. I sat at home in a kind of stupor. Life did not interest me. I went nowhere, saw no one. Though her energies were now occupied mostly with Rennie, Mona tried to draw me out. Would I like to go with them to a party, to the movies? It was well meant, but I could not help feeling resentful. I began to believe that Mona enjoyed mothering me for the power it gave her. Now that she was with Rennie, the role of protector was hers undisputed. We were no longer equals in our difficulties with men; she had broken through to the other side, leaving me to flounder on my own. I declined her invitations, giving in only when loneliness threatened to swamp me completely. Even then, their company did not soothe me; I felt a nervous emptiness, as if they were the parents and I were the child. Each of these encounters I left determined never to be drawn in again. But then I would give in, and the whole cycle started up again as if it had never stopped.

There began to be a certain insistence in Mona's invitations. If I could not come to a party with them, surely I would come for dinner? And if not dinner, would I like to go for drinks after work? If I wanted to meet her in private, she demanded that Rennie be included. I wondered if it had gotten so bad between them that they could not bear to be alone together and needed a third party to keep from flying apart, like opposing charges. But the weight of my own mysterious misery had dragged me down too far to think very clearly about Mona and Rennie, or even to care.

Gradually, I cut myself off from them. Two weeks, a month passed. Then one evening Mona called. "It's all over between Rennie and me," she said. "It feels so much better to be free.' I did not know whether to offer sympathy or congratulations. We made plans to meet the next day for lunch.

Later that evening there was a tap on my door. It was Rennie. "May I come in?" he said. He sat on my living room floor smoking cigarettes. "It's all over between Mona and me," he said. "She made the most impossible demands. I'm so glad it's over." He seemed lighthearted and cheery, puffing on his cigarette. "How hospitable you are," he said. "Mona always made me smoke on the porch. Can you imagine, she once had a temper tantrum because I would not read so-and-so's book?"

I knew the book well. Mona and I had used it as a touchstone of our personal philosophy. But I had to laugh at her naïve determination to educate Rennie. Mona herself was none too sure of her ground in the world of letters. I said as much to Rennie. He laughed too. "You are so understanding," he said later, as he was leaving.

The next day I saw Mona. She did not mention Rennie, and I decided it would not be tactful to tell her of his visit. Mona was full of other interests. She had met some potters through a ceramics class she was taking and was eager to throw herself, as it were, into this new activity. Once again I saw her posed to plunge into a venture she hoped would provide her life with meaning. I realized we had grown apart. Conversation lagged. We parted with no definite plans to meet again.

Two nights later Rennie called. "Are you and Mona back together yet?" I teased. "Of course not," he said. "I called to invite you to dinner." I was amused that Rennie did not seem to be conforming to the role of rejected lover. "This is too fast," I said. "I don't believe you and Mona are entirely through with each other. I have no intention of entering a triangle with you. If you and she have really broken off for good, I will go out with you, but not before." "But we have," he said. "It needs more time," I replied. Rennie said, "I guess you're right," and rang off. He sounded discouraged.

I congratulated myself on my prudence. Secretly, I was amazed at my own behavior. For various reasons it came as no surprise that Rennie was interested in me. But I had never been attracted to him, with or without Mona. My feelings toward both of them had cooled. Why had I promised to see him at all?

Rennie was persistent. He phoned me twice more the following week. I put him off. I began to understand how Mona had felt, courted by him. It was not unpleasant.

Mona called one Friday. She talked at length about ceramics. Before hanging up, she said, "I can't tell you how good it feels to be out of this situation with Rennie. I was being suffocated. I hope he's not taking it too badly." Again I was poised to bring up the matter of his phone calls. But since she was making her adjustment so well, why mention it? Her vanity would be offended. I said nothing.

Saturday night Rennie appeared at my door with a bottle of wine. I realized that without ever making a conscious decision to do so, I had started to "see" him. I watched as he wrestled with the bottle and a corkscrew in my kitchen. He still did not arouse me.

Rennie reminded me of a flounder that does a few half-hearted flops on the dock when you reel it in—someone who consulted a paperback horoscope in his bathroom and wondered if anybody liked him. With these thoughts running through my head, I went to bed with him that night He was not a floppy flounder, but when I woke up in the morning I was confused. I did not know what I felt.

Rennie assumed it was the start of a wonderful affair and came to see me every night. I began to see why he was so popular with women. I let myself be carried motionless on the wings of his enthusiasm. He compared me constantly to Mona. "You are so calm and understanding. You are not neurotic, you know what you want." Then he began to understand that although I was curious up to a point, I did not exactly welcome such comparisons and discreetly he dropped them.

How to broach the subject to Mona became more and more a problem as the first weeks of our liaison slipped by. Rennie said, "She was so rude and crude the last time we met I have no desire to see her or think of her again." "But she is so easily hurt," I said. "It's only fair that she be told. Since you parted for good, and each of you is happily going his own way, why should it matter?" I saw no reason why the three of us could not be friends once again, even if on a rather different basis. Rennie finally agreed. "But you should be the one to tell her," he said. "Often, when the three of us were together, I felt left out. I was jealous of the close communion between you and Mona."

The next time Mona called, we spoke of various things. Then I said, "Rennie and I have been seeing each other, you know." There was a pause on the line. Then Mona said, "How very strange." I said, "Don't worry, it's strictly casual." Mona said, "I'm not worried." I said, "Good." And we left it at that.

When I told Rennie of our conversation, he laughed bitterly. "You watch," he said. "Now that her vanity is involved, she will decide she was madly in love with me all along." I laughed too, but had to reproach him. "You speak as if she were a bad person." He said, "I know her well." Privately I felt that Rennie had seen only a small side of Mona's personality. That was the problem with sexual connections, they were the intensest but also the narrowest way of knowing another person. Other situations revealed other selves a lover could never guess at.

It was true that Rennie knew me scarcely at all. I told him very little about myself, having no desire to exhibit my thoughts and feelings to him. Why it should be so, I could not say. Perhaps it was because he had the habit of declaring he was passionately in love with me, in a way that made me believe and disbelieve him all at once. He would often begin some remark or other by saying, "If we were married—." Those are the words that stick in most men's throats, but Rennie pronounced them with indecent ease. Could he actually be sincere? I said to him, "You are starting this affair in the middle, not at the beginning." He looked hurt, bewildered, as if to say, how petty of you to spoil a tender sentiment!

I did not know what to think.

One day we had an argument about Mona. "She is such a limited person," Rennie said. I said, "She is not." I did not tell him Mona was now making frequent phone calls to find out what was happening between him and me. In spite of my assurances that it was a low-key affair, she had begun to sound hurt and unsure of herself. One time she even burst into tears. I had stolen her man, she said. I felt guilty and angry at the same time. It was certainly true that I hadn't waited the decent interval I had promised myself. On the other hand, Mona had always given the impression that she considered Rennie unworthy of her attention. She had said she was glad to be rid of him. Our conversation ended in confusion and bad feelings. I thought about it for several days. Obviously, my judgment of their relationship had been misguided. Rennie had not been in love with Mona. Mona had been in love with Rennie, and he had resisted her efforts to make him over in her image. Therefore Mona was actually the hurt party, and I had compounded the difficulties by taking up so quickly with her former lover.

I said to Rennie, "Mona is upset. Perhaps you

owe her an apology." Since his feelings for her were so definitely ended, I felt I ran no risk in offering this suggestion. He had only that day proposed that we travel together to Yucatan the following month. I said, "Wouldn't it be better to end on a peaceful note instead of bitterness all around?"

He resisted a bit, then said, "Very well. I will go get the rest of my clothes from her house tomorrow and perhaps we can settle it so that no one is sad."

The next day he came to my house and said, "Well, that's done. You were right, as usual. Now we can let it lie in peace." After that he did not call for several days, which was unusual. Then he called and said, "We must get together Sunday night, at least for dinner." There was an odd note in his voice, as if he were speaking to an invalid. I said, "Is something wrong?" He hesitated, then said, "You should know that Mona and I are seeing each other again." I felt a surge of anger. "Why?" He said, "Well, we were always very close, you know." I said, "I told you at the beginning I had no desire to enter a triangle with you and Mona. Those were the conditions. What have you done?" He said nothing. With a fury that rose from some hidden place, I said, "You two are like dogs licking your own vomit," and hung up.

For three weeks I heard nothing from either of them. The relation between Rennie and me had evaporated as quickly as it had begun. I was not angry with him. Rennie was so passive, what could you expect? It was Mona who received the full force of my feelings. I grew to hate her with a slow, smoldering rage, each resentment feeding the next. Meanwhile a small part of me whispered that I had not loved Rennie at all, why was I so hurt by this new turn of events? There was no rational explanation for my feelings.

One day I met Mona in a store. Paralyzed by the force of my anger, I said nothing. Mona was sweet and considerate. She said she wanted to return the money she owed me. Would it be better to send it by mail? In the early days with Rennie, Mona had gotten pregnant. She hadn't wanted Rennie to know about it and borrowed the money from me to have her pregnancy terminated. I had forgotten about Mona's abortion until the time she had called me on the phone to cry and accuse me of stealing her man. She spoke of the pain she had felt having an abortion. That was why I had felt guilty and sent Rennie to make amends.

In a choked voice, I requested her to deliver the money in person.

Later that afternoon she knocked on my door. I had rehearsed what I would say to her. When she had taken a seat, I said, "Why were you always throwing the three of us together, Mona? I think all along you must have been after me, not Rennie. You think that having Rennie so soon after he was with me is a way of having me. As matters stand now, you will probably catch my chlamydia. Is that what you wanted? It isn't what I wanted, and that is why I left Rennie as soon as he told me he was seeing you again."

Mona flinched. I knew I had struck at her deepest reined-in desire, one she had never voiced but that I had been able to guess over the months of our friendship. She waited a moment until she composed herself. "No, that is not what I wanted. I confess, I am a manipulating female. Rennie has always gone after other women, it is his constant habit. I felt you would be less of a threat than some of my other women friends who are more attractive."

I laughed, loudly.

Without changing expression, Mona continued. "Since he was bound to sleep with someone close to me to get revenge, I thought it was safer for him to do it with you, because then it would be easier for me to get him back."

I watched in silence as she put the check on my desk, along with a sweater she had borrowed months before. She had already walked out the door and was in her car when I realized it was too late to catch up with her. I wanted to grab her by the hair and beat her face to a pulp. Then I would kick her body into a gravel pit. Then—my hands clenched into fists. They stayed that way for days. I could not sleep at night because of the violent fantasies running through my brain.

Two weeks later, Rennie called me. "Would you like to have dinner at my house?" he said. I laughed bitterly. "You and Mona must be having a quarrel." Rennie made an exasperated noise. "You made a free choice," he reminded me. "I'm only calling because I want to see you again." This made me hesitate. I cared nothing for Rennie, but he was offering me a chance to salve my injured pride. It was a golden opportunity to avenge myself on Mona. But something stopped me. "It must be your father that makes you this way," I said. I had met his father. "My father?" said Rennie. "Yes," I said, "if you were not so afraid of his tyranny you would not be making so many women miserable." Rennie's voice was weary. "I am sick to death of you and Mona psychoanalyzing me." I hung up.

The following week I heard through friends that Mona and Rennie had parted for good. Three months later Rennie married a quiet girl from a wealthy family and they bought a house in the country. He sees other women, of course, but his wife either knows nothing or tolerates it.

Mona and I were left as we were before, alone and adrift, this time totally at odds with each other. Mona went into therapy. I took up white water rafting. Her viciousness, the unfairness of it all, still deeply upset me.

I was surprised, whenever we met in public, to see my own anger reflected back from Mona's scornful eyes. What did she have to be upset about? She had gotten Rennie back. That she lost him again came through no interference of mine. If what she had said to me that day was true, then all along she had successfully manipulated me to her advantage. I had been outmaneuvered and outranked down the line. Her schemes, her pretenses, her overwhelming weaknesses—what was my sin in the face of all that?

I had a dream. In the dream I held a shotgun and blasted Mona again and again in the face and chest. Sobbing and clutching the gun, I cried, "Mona, I love you! Don't die." From the ground, dying, Mona said, "Go away, I hate you. Now you are more beautiful than I am."

I had been waiting to hear those words, it seems—for as soon as she spoke them, I woke up in a burst of shameful happiness.

Blonde Is Blonde
(But Silver Runs Deep)

I, Vilvea, declare everything that follows is true.

The problem is the mirror. My downstairs hall mirror is haunted. Three times I turn to look into it and what do I see? Not my own neat features and long brown tresses. Three times a stranger's face simpers back, a cheap common waitress person with a potato nose and a blonde bouffant. And is that my lovely furniture behind the hateful face—couch and chairs shabby and stained, ashtrays overflowing, lipstick smeared on the carpet?

So I'm walking down the street when a total stranger comes up to me. I don't remember much about her except that she is blonde. She says to me, "My whole life changed when I dyed my hair." She says, "Men showered me with attention."

I am on my way to Walmart, where I buy a bottle of my favorite shampoo. When I get home, I wash my hair with it. My hair turns blonde. So I take another look at the label on the bottle. Peroxide. In the Walmart store I must have mistaken shampoo for peroxide. How flashy I must look. What an embarrassing mistake. Everyone will think I did it to draw attention to myself.

Then I look in the downstairs hall mirror. The peroxide must have been too strong. My hair is not blonde. It's silver all over.

So I go back to Walmart, buy a blonde rinse, take it home and try it.

A perfect blonde.

I go back to Walmart, which is full of women who crowd around me in great excitement when they find I have dyed my hair blonde. A farm girl, fat and brown haired, pushes forward to tell me about her own experiences. I cut her off. I would rather talk to the salesgirl, who has single blonde strands elegantly plaited into braids in her long brown hair.

But I never get a chance to learn how she does it. Instead, I find myself explaining to this audience of women that I have a lot of silver, underneath this blonde. Blonde dye reacts differently to silver than to ordinary hair, I tell them. I look into a sea of blank faces. Nobody understands.

On my way back from Walmart I see a kind-looking man sitting in a booth in a tea shop. So I go in and show the man a picture of myself, my new self, all blonde and smiling. "Vilvea looks sad," he says. Outraged, I stalk away. Can't he see how hard she's smiling?

Then I pass a woman in the street wearing a gold filigree ring on her finger. I try to remember the ring a man once gave me that I lost. This lost ring wasn't filigree. It was solid silver.

Home at last. In the downstairs hall mirror my blonde hair is loaded with flakes of dandruff.

Big event. The income from my family investments dries up. I am forced out on the streets in search of work. So I become a scrubwoman—at Walmart.

It isn't as bad as it sounds. The head scrubwoman is eighty years old, eight feet tall and eight months pregnant. Her hair is white as snow. She and I work in a large deserted warehouse among rows and rows of great tall shelves full of merchandise. Right off, I notice the bottles of hair dye arranged in tiers. Each bottle has the following notice on its label.

"Every woman in America who is not a teenager or a derelict should dye her hair when silver begins to show."

When I read this out loud, the head scrubwoman laughs. "My hair turned silver when I was twenty," she says.

I get home from work and look in the downstairs hall mirror. A fat bourgeois matron with a blonde and henna-streaked permanent wave stares back.

So I sit down to watch television. Who should be on but Marilyn Monroe? "How do you like being Marilyn Monroe?" says the interviewer. "Fine," says Marilyn Monroe. "But when you're like this"—she touches her cropped blonde locks—"You always wish you were dark haired and passionate."

Right after Marilyn Monroe comes a show called "The Girl with the Brown Eyes."

The opening scene is a clearing in the forest, where the group of women from the Walmart store are gathered. They're all looking up. From the top of the tree at the edge of the clearing a woman leaps. Supported by the gauzy wings attached to her velvet coat, she drifts lazily to the ground. It is the fat farm girl who tried to tell me something. The other women surround her joyfully as she lands. One of them cries, "Would you look at her hair?"

I look. What a miracle. The girl flier's hair is all silver and brown.

Just then a noise comes from the basement. I go down the kitchen stairs, shining my flashlight ahead on each step. At the bottom of the stairwell sits a decaying straw basket. In the basket an ancient yellow cat both male and female nurses a tiny kitten. The old cat's face is covered with a transparent caul of afterbirth. Its mouth smirks over long teeth and receding gums. The old cat thinks a thought that I receive.

"That which I am, you are not nor will be."

I climb back up the stairs and look in the hall mirror. Vilvca looks back. I think to myself.

Blonde is blonde, but silver runs deep.

Wild Child

Deep in the woodsy woods, a few crisp leaves and dry twigs snapping underfoot, here and there the print of a deer hoof—that's where I am one bright October morning when a thicket near the trail starts shaking. Out she bursts and stands before me, all two feet of her, curly brown hair and brown eyes, naked, a gold locket around her neck. She grins, she giggles. She stretches out her pudgy arms. Without thinking I lift her up and take her home with me, which was clearly her intention.

    The lovingest little girl a new mother could ask for, that's my wild child. These first few years we're inseparable. I teach her how to talk and she's an eager pupil. Of her past only two signs remain: the gold locket shaped like a heart, which opens up to reveal a space for a photograph, but none is there; and her poor little private parts, which she does not let me touch when I bathe her. The tiny lips are sealed shut, crusted with a dark dried substance. But the doctor she refuses entirely to see, giving me to understand with signs and words she will vanish from my life forever if I try to force her to.

    So I do nothing. It's wrong of me, it's selfish not

to insist, but I hope to let her heal by herself, within herself. Slowly during her baths the crusted substance dissolves, the lips part to their natural position and look entirely healthy. Later I will understand she has not healed at all, that I have not helped her when she needed me to. She's so very strong willed, that's my excuse. Her will was always stronger than mine, that's what I believe, but later I will see all the ways I imposed my own on her.

Because the signs are so ambiguous, so fraught with unspoken danger, together we conspire to push away my wild child's past. There is only us, and the future. My goal? To tame her, civilize her, bring her splendidly into the world.

In my mission I succeed all too well .As my child grows, her innocent wildness turns to worldly willfulness. She tastes power. She likes it. Watching her success, I change too, sensing inside the stirrings of a feeling foreign to our earlier bliss. Envy. I envy her. So that she won't seem to surpass me, I look for faults in my beloved wild child, traits to take her to task for—but silently, in my heart, I can never reproach her directly.

Now she's a popular, ambitious adolescent. She thinks about schools and careers and important people to know. And in this blossoming black flower I recognize, reluctantly, the tightly closed bud inside my own heart. She takes after me. The animal fierceness I have so admired is focused now, in a way that does not please me but has somehow, coming from me, infected her. Her beauty is pressed into service, so is the genuineness that has now become a strategy. I tell myself I don't like these things in her only because secretly I want them too, these fruits of her ambition.

Even with these changes, my wild child and I stay entwined. I listen to her adventures, praise her triumphs, encourage her schemes. She decides on a show business life. And she is mightily successful, beyond my wishes and her dreams. Once in motion, it's a steamroller that picks up momentum and can't stop until it turns into celebrity. I fade into her background. It's too much, even for that black bud in my heart.

Visiting her dressing room the one time, I knock and enter, but her bare back stays turned. In the mirror the beautiful painted face glares at me.

I come right to the point. "What's the matter? This is what you wanted."

"It's not what *I* wanted. It's only what my injury demanded—as recompense. Inside me all is blasted and dead. Why else do you think I perverted my nature in this grotesque way? It's your fault. Why did you ignore my injury?"

"I am sorry. I am so sorry. But you did not let me touch you. You did not let me take you to the doctor. You would not tell me what happened to you. How could I help you when you would not let me?"

"You should have made me tell you. You should have made me go to the doctor, not that the doctor would have helped. You should not have accepted my silence."

"Well, tell me now."

"I can't tell you because I don't know."

"You don't know how that happened?"

"Once I had a dream. Someone driving a car hit my cat and killed her. At the last moment I turned my head away. Why watch my cat die when I only want to remember how beautiful she was alive?

"And the rest of your past?"

"I don't remember."

"You remember nothing?"

"Nothing."

I sigh. What can I do to help her now? When I ask her this directly, her body quivers with energy, rage, and life. Turning to face me for the first time, she reaches into her purse, a gypsy bag made of scraps of faded cloth and bangles most unsuited to her stylish new life. She pulls out an object and hands it to me. "Take my mirror."

I take the small black frame. There's nothing in it, not even a piece of glass. "It's not a mirror," I say. "It's an empty picture frame."

"Hold it up." She guides my hand so that the frame is midway between our faces. I look through it at her. She looks through it at me.

"It's a mirror," she says. "Be my wild child now."

I consider. I found her and I raised her, if inadequately. I've fulfilled my responsibilities. Now I'm free to be her wild child.

I say, "Yes."

With nothing holding me back, nothing to stop my glorious bolt, I plunge into the forest and make it my home. In my nakedness, wearing her gold locket, I eat bulbs and acorns and wild grasses. I talk to the other animals. I sleep in the rooty troughs of huge old trees.

I pass weeks and weeks in the woods.

One day a leathery-skinned boy with long dangling arms show up. He leads me on a faint track through the trees to a clearing where a mound of earth is all heaped up. A cleft runs deep down the middle of this mound, which is rock hard even though it's made of soil.

"Lie down in the furrow," the boy said. So I clamber up the hard oval mound and lie in the cramped narrow fissure. With my back bowed in its curve, I fall asleep.

Before me stands buxom Mother Nature, bespectacled and elderly. "Here's a strange sight," she says, and steps aside to show me a homeless man lying on the ground. The head of a second man, whom he has somehow managed to swallow whole, sticks out of the homeless man's mouth. The swallowed-up man's mouth holds another head still. A woman's, talking and talking. This chattering female head, this woman, seems to have no idea of her predicament.

Hard light glints off Mother Nature's wire-rimmed glasses. "She's twice swallowed, can't you see? Get her out of those gullets."

But how? I grab the first man's ankles and pull. Out of his mouth, lizardlike, slides the full body of the second man with the woman's head still engorged. So I grab this man's ankles and pull again. The woman's body slips out easily, encased in shiny goo. I drag her to a little clear pond and wash the slime off her body. All this time the head gabbles on.

"Be quiet!" I say finally. She stops talking while I rinse her. When I'm done, I lead the silent woman by the hand through the woods until we reach the mound in the clearing. Then her body becomes my body and I'm lying on the mound, which starts to shake and quiver.

The leathery-skinned boy claps his hands sharply and I wake up.

I climb down from the mound and walk back alone to my part of the forest. What does my dream mean? Is it supposed to heal me, heal my wild child? All I know is this. I'm howling. I'm standing here howling, deep in the woodsy woods where only she can find me, and here I'll stay, stay, stay—till she comes back for me.

If the Earth Quakes

Earthquakes heave up from below.
    Earthquakes destroy shaky structures.
    Earthquakes bring the dead to life.
    If the earth quakes when I am sitting in my study and my books topple on me, I will not survive the upset. I must live in all my house.
    If the earth quakes when I am in my bedroom with my love and the floor drops out from under us, I will not survive the upset. To survive the upset I must live in all my house.
    If the earth quakes before I have crossed a bridge and it destroys that bridge, I will not grow up.
    If I jump in the water, I protect myself with ignorance. If I tread in place, I will not know I have not grown up.
    If the sidewalk cracks open to reveal an abyss, I must not jump into it.
    If the abyss releases a flock of birds, I must not fly away with them. But if the birds light down in a tree near my house, I must attend to that tree.
    If the tree flowers, I rejoice.
    If the tree dies, I plant another.
    I leave the water. I build a bridge and cross it.
    I inhabit my whole house.

Jacob's Ladder

Sumac and Rigger

The whole business, I don't know quite what else to call it, starts with the old woman. She comes to me with a basket of rare herbs she has gathered in the forbidden forest. She has come to give the herbs to me.

The old woman points to each plant in the basket and tells me its name.

"What is that one?" I ask. It looks like a stalk of wheat.

I am embarrassed to be caught out in my ignorance.

"And these new spices," she says with special emphasis, "are *sumac* and *rigger*. You have never seen them before."

I peer into the basket, but nothing registers.

The Red-Haired Thief

The next installment takes place in London. The red-haired thief terrorizes the city with his daring exploits. Women know he has broken into their rooms because he always leaves behind a bunch of red roses. By that sign I understand that he is not really a bad man.

Every night I lie in bed in my Bloomsbury flat waiting for the red-haired thief to break into my room with his roses. He never comes. He has never come. He will never come. It's because I failed to recognize sumac and rigger.

Sprouts
You can't imagine my despair when the red-haired thief refused to show up. It threw me back on myself, so to speak. Now I am convinced that without that loss, without that failure, the rest would never have happened. All the time I kept thinking, what happened to me? How did I lose the vision? What happened to the little girl?

La Belle Chanteuse
Resplendent in white opera gloves and a black lamé evening gown, she sings her heart out for the absent love of her torch song. The only thing a bit out of the ordinary is that fact that she is standing on her head on a chair. "*Regardez moi,*" she sings to me, with a peculiar whining twist on the *moi.*

I watch her in helpless amazement. How can she tell me to *regardez*, when she is hogging the only dress of its kind in the world? And I am such an ugly little girl.

Milton the Menacing
Down by the old playground, past the high plywood

fence plastered with old circus handbills—wild animals, trapeze artists, Sheena the Jungle Girl—I skip along in my saddle shoes, happy as a clam. I am back in my rightful world, no more bothersome reminders of la belle chanteuse to torment my mind. But it is "out of the frying pan and into the fire."

This is the world of Milton the Menacing.

Crouched behind the fence, he lies in wait for me. He knows this is the way I always come home from school. Milton the Menacing has mean, snarly teeth and ugly eyes, big hulking body and small, stumpy hands. With a hideous growl, he jumps poor unsuspecting me at the corner. As he bites my neck, I scream and scream.

My Ship Sinks

Kind of a clunky old tub, but mine own. On it I have sailed the seven seas, but I won't bore you with the interminable adventures of a female sailor. Believe me, they are many, and complex beyond belief.

An interesting incident takes place just outside the Copenhagen harbor. My good old boat springs a leak. In seconds flat, it sinks beneath the waves. A shock, after all that time on the bounding main. But the biggest surprise is yet to come.

We drift to the bottom of the sea in a cloud of bubbles and settle with a plop on the sandy bottom.

Lo and behold, there are people down here.

Nobody I recognize, it's a whole new crowd. In

fact, none of them seem to have faces. To my embarrassment, I can't distinguish one of the undersea people from another. Surely they'll think I'm prejudiced.

I hide out in the hold of my ship at the bottom of the sea.

A Respite
There is a river with jungly banks and beautiful dark water. People float on it, kissing and hugging each other. They are not floating downstream, they are being pulled up, up, up to the source.

Kill-Crazy
Nothing much happens to me for a time. But the whatever-you-call-it is full of surprises. All of a sudden I am an Amazon princess with a spear and a golden headdress.

Have you any idea how this makes me feel, after so much humiliation and defeat? I am drunk with power, a glorious feeling. My women obey me without question. The jungle lies at my feet.

You see, the civilized world was destroying itself with wars and conflict. I cut off all contact with them years ago to preserve the life of my tribe. We have avoided the contagion of their misery. My women and I make love upon ourselves. I have three concubines.

One day we come upon a man in the forest

where no man has set foot in years. I cut off his head and throw it to the dogs. With a knife of iron I cut the pumping heart out of his body, spit it, and roast it on the open fire. In the flames it swells like a marshmallow, crusty and black.

Suddenly, in the height of my power, a sharp grief pierces me. I cry bitter tears.

Turkey in the Straw
Not a big bird lying on the floor—a dance! But so much still eludes me!

Will I Ever Learn?
When she returns in the night, the old woman is brusque. "I am going to tell you a story," she says. "Be quiet and listen."

Listen? *Regardez?* "It will be a lesson," I say, "And I will have to understand it or be cursed a thousand years."

"Not a *lesson*," the old woman says fiercely. "Be quiet. I am giving it to you."

And this was the tale.

The Three Fishermen
Once upon a time in the middle of nowhere there was a little lake, fed by three wide waterfalls pouring over a green cliff. Into the lake three fishermen cast their lines.

The first fisherman caught a big black fish, the

second caught a little golden fish, and the third, with great effort, landed the rotten hull of an old fishing scow. (Much laughter from his companions.) But when the boat was beached, it began to sprout great green vines whose tendrils crept over the ground in all directions.

The black fish turned into a crow with white legs and flew away.

They cooked the golden fish over a fire and ate it—bones, tail, and all. By the time they had finished, the boat had spawned a noble forest of tall trees, with little birds hopping on branches and deer peeking through the twisted brush.

The three fishermen walked into the forest. Their feet trod softly on the matted leaves and ferns. Dense green growth hid the sky. After they had gone a little way, the black crow with white legs swooped out of the trees and lit on the first fisherman's shoulder. Into his ear this sly, French-speaking crow whispered secrets of the forest. Together they took to the trails and vanished from sight.

The second and third fishermen continued on their way, stopping to admire the strange plants that grew in this forbidden forest. Then the yellow witch stepped out of a flowering herb to claim the fisherman that caught the golden fish. With one stroke, she bit off his head with her sharp teeth and spun a cocoon of golden cobwebs around it. "This one will not wake up for seven years," she laughed.

The third fisherman walked on, oppressed by his solitude in the forest and the fate of his companions. In the midst of his sorrow, he came upon a little stream of running water.

Crossing the Stream
I am on the other side. "Come to me, cross the stream," I say. "It's been a long and weary wait."

The third fisherman hovers on the bank, looking at me, then plunges in. A terrible thing happens: when his feet touch the water, they dissolve to foam. His legs evaporate, then his torso. "Help me, help me!' he cries.

Desperately, I stretch out my arms to him. I grasp his hands. For a moment they are strong and firm.

"Too late!" he cries. His hands let go of mine, and the fisherman vanishes into the racing foam that slips away down the stream.

I run along the bank calling to him, cursing the old woman and my fate, trying to keep pace with the racing water. But I come out under sunny skies on top of the cliff, and I am looking over one of the three waterfalls that pours into the little lake.

A red ruby glistens in the rocks at the edge of the precipice—all that's left of the third fisherman.

I take it because it's mine, and the thing is finished.

A Bestiary of My Heart

Dangerous Animals
My purpose is to tell of bodies changed into shapes of a different kind. When I was a little girl, animals were my enemies. Sharks shredded me. Grizzlies rent me. Tigers sprang out of the dead grass. Rattlesnakes bit and bit me.

All that I got used to, strange to say. I thought it was the way things were. I thought it was the way things always would be. But it wasn't. Other things happened. It's different now.

The Empty Lot
Summer of my twelfth year, strolling in the empty weed-filled lot below the house, I bend down to pick a daisy. A rattlesnake coiled around the stem rears up to strike. I step back. The field erupts. Rattlesnakes, hundreds of them in boiling motion. By force of will I rise off the ground, I hover ten feet above the hissing snakes that carpet the hard dirt. If I lose my concentration for even a moment, I'll fall and be bitten to death.

Sharkbait

Same setup with the sharks and the deer. Here's a sunny day, stags and does swimming in the warm waters of the Gulf Stream. The invisible shark attacks. No one can see him, we know him by the marks he leaves. Bright gouts of blood marble the deep green sea. Bleeding carcasses litter the beach.

I go fishing for the shark. From up in the stratosphere where I've put myself I snag the creature. With my fishhook made from a human legbone, I reel him in. Then fall, fall, fall thousands of feet to meet my catch. Land the shark, understand, the moment I hit water.

Next time I fish for the shark, he swallows the hook and tows me miles and miles through an underwater tunnel into the light.

Third time, he's completely different. He has human eyes.

The new shark leaps over the bowsprit onto the deck of our fishing scow. "This means trouble," I tell my learned female friend. "We'll need to move fast to get out of the way."

We don't move fast. Slowly, slowly we back up a step or two. The little white shark flip-flops on the varnished boards of the deck. Small but solid, he looks at us with impossibly pretty eyes.

I say again, "We'll have to move fast."

Slowly, slowly we walk backward through the cabin to the stern. Below us the water roils. Up leaps the shark over the railings. He lands squirming at our feet.

"This shark is dangerous," I tell my friend. The shark looks at us. We look at him. His eyes have lids and lashes.

We move to another boat. And another. Shutting cabin doors, putting up barricades.

I say, "Dangerous."

Panther-Parrot

Compared to snakes and sharks, cats are a piece of cake. Even big ones.

Night falls on the Indian subcontinent. A group of us ride elephants through the countryside. Gratefully I climb off my mount, a practical way to travel but oh so slow, uncomfortable too. I get separated from the others and now I'm alone in the jungle.

A saber-tooth cat blacker than the shadows stalks me through the trees. But I'm not afraid anymore. So it melts into a small growling dun-colored bobcat running toward me. I hold my ground. I snarl just as fiercely.

Really, I give quite a good snarl.

Things happen fast now. My snarling turns the bobcat into a little monkey who leaps up and perches on my shoulder. The monkey becomes a parrot chattering in my ear. In all that gibberish I make out scraps of words, real words it's learned by heart from humans. Words in a language I still don't understand.

Black Leather Cat

I take the lesson: better to be a scary animal than to meet one. And this is just as true of cities as the Indian jungle.

The other night, for instance. A young blonde woman complained to me her boyfriend was treating her bad. So I put on my black leather coat and pants. I put on my black leather cat head with its vinyl whiskers. I picked up my black leather rod.

Now I was a black leather cat. And I taught that fellow a thing or two.

Cat Hospital

But cats have problems, too. Three men and a woman in white coats sit at a long table stitching up cut-open cats, a surgical assembly line. At the end of the table the woman clamps an oxygen mask on the striped orange muzzle of an enormous tiger.

To this cat hospital I bring my two domestic kittens. One is orange and one is black. A doctor tells me they have *hydroangioencephalitis*—that is, brain and heart rabies—because they were bitten by a rat. (Snake, I think, but close enough.) I know they are being cared for here in the cat hospital. But will my poor pusses ever get well?

My grown cat swims across the estuary and dives into a heap of trash. He catches a rat, kills it. Large armadillos lumber through my living room. They're after that big grey rat who just jumped out of my old Shakespeare book, the rat I don't see creeping along the sofa, about to bite my neck from behind.

All rats are not bad. I know of a few that turned into kittens. But they were ugly kittens.

Between my cat and the armadillos, many rats are slain.

Beasts of the Air

Two days of the year my coastal town is full of monarch butterflies. One fall day the monarchs pass through going south, one spring day they pass through coming back. My cat scoops them out of the air by the pawful, brings the delicate-winged bodies into the house for me to admire. I drop the ragged orange and black scraps off the second-story porch. Some scraps fall straight to the ground and lie there, others flutter away. They do not die, but they are changed.

A young man with long white hair shows me a magic tree with red bees buzzing in it, plump red bees with black stripes on their bodies. Where's the hive?

Over there, out of sight in the leafy branches.

Boa-Boa

Big multicolored snakes slide restlessly across the floor of my tiny room. Why won't anybody kill them?

Deep in the woods lies a cave. In the cave lives a giant snake. The snake draws me like a magnet. I wait at the entrance, reverently. A shape moves out of the darkness. The swollen, reared-up head wears a golden crown. Bow down to King Cobra.

Four men play poker at a kitchen table. The host owns a boa constrictor that has disappeared. Long burlap curtains heave at the window. The boa, bored and hungry, has crawled up the sill, slipped, and caught a fang in the burlap. He's dangling like a living pull-cord and he's plenty mad. But they're all too drunk to unlatch him.

My female friend has a cat and a boa constrictor in her house that I must care for. I feed the cat, forget about the boa constrictor. Then I find him in her closet, hanging snaggle-toothed next to her scarves. He drops to the floor. Now he's a gorgeous emerald green lizard. He has legs. What if he crawled under the bed? I shut the closet door fast, but the lock is broken.

A man. It seems he is my lover, I know nothing about it. This man releases boa constrictors into every stream in the county. Too late to stop him, the damage is done. The snakes fill the streams to the brim. Water spills over and floods the countryside. All my labors for nothing, the snakes are coming. Snakes and people, we're all being swept out to sea!

Ring of Light
In the Gulf Stream waters directly off that beach of carnage the beasts swim round and round and I swim with them–snakes and elephants, cats and monkeys and sharks, even a guy on his motorcycle, won't it get rusty? The ocean sparkles. Gulls wheel and dive through clouds of horseflies and wasps. The blood washes off my body.

My friend, have you heard the music of the spheres? In the split-second before the circle breaks, before we revert to warring elements, the spheres sound one majestic chord, *harmonium*!

Praise to the life in all of us.

CPSIA information can be obtained at www.ICGtesting.com
Printed in the USA
BVOW021332171111

276301BV00001B/2/P